GERALDINE RYAN-LUSH

GOODBYE WART!

Written By Geraldine Ryan-Lush

(c)Copyright Geraldine Ryan-Lush 2019

Illustrated By Doriano Strologo (c) Copyright Doriano Strologo 2019

Illustrated By Geraldine Ryan-Lush (c) Copyright Geraldine Ryan-Lush 2019

Cover Art by Doriano Strologo

Published by Mulberry Books

ISBN 978-0-9947339-9-3

For Lyla and Riley. Also in memory of Kathleen Marie Power

Ryan, whose artwork circa 1936 appears in this book.

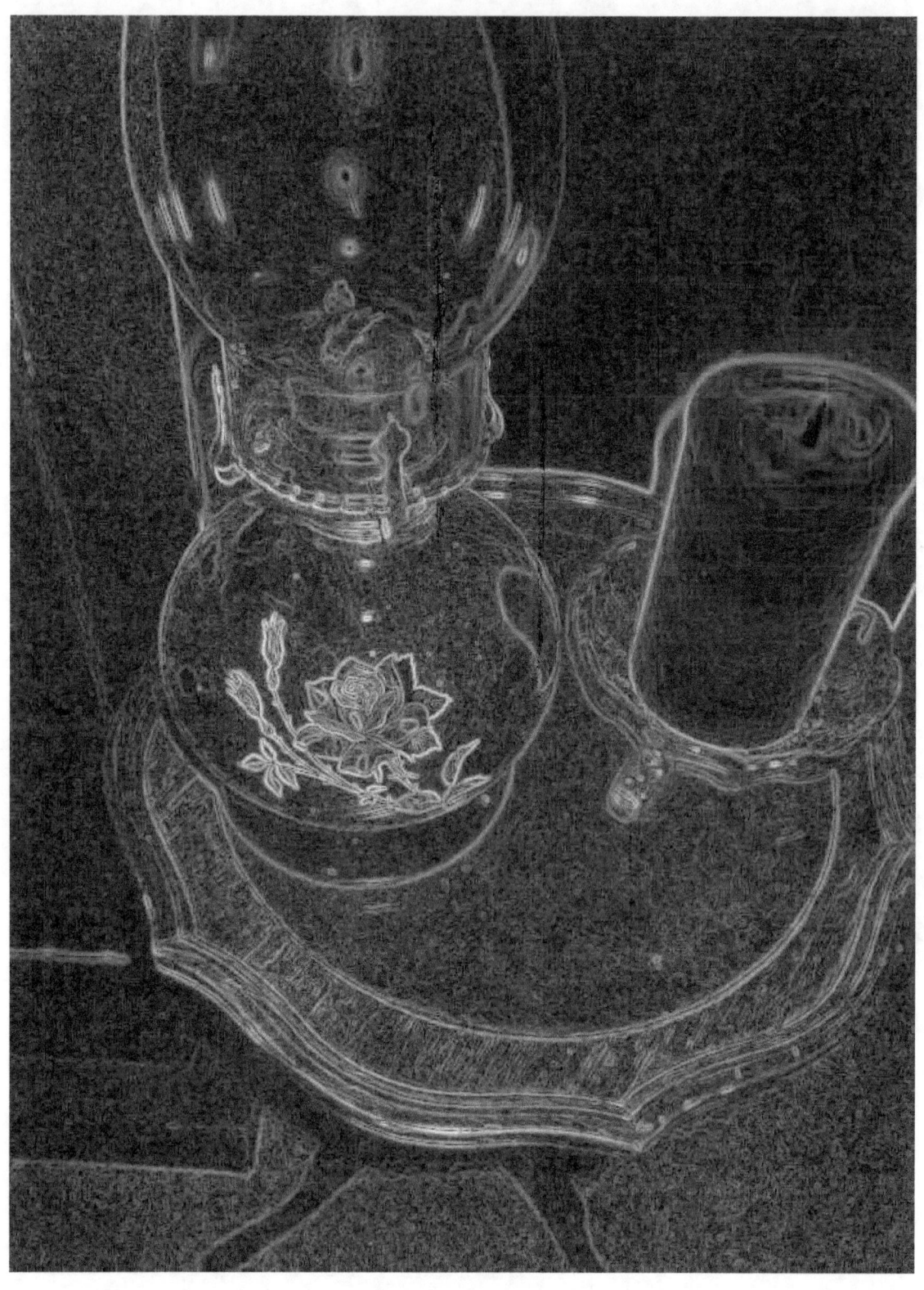

I had a Wart

An Ugly Wart

A Not So Very Funny Wart

Right on my middle finger.

It wasn't Tiny,

Wasn't Shiny,

Like normal Warts would be.

It was a Gross and Awful Wart

A Mean and Green and Hateful Wart

This Grimey, Slimey, Blimey Wart

That went EVERYWHERE with me!

It stuck on tight with all its might

And looked real Scary in the night.

It was indeed a Gruesome Sight

This Mean and Green and Hateful Wart

This Not So Friendly, Ugly Wart

This Not So Tiny, Not So Shiny

Throbbing, Bobbing, Knobbly, Wobbly

Fat and so Unkindly Wart

That went EVERYWHERE with me!

I wanted to Destroy the Wart

To say, "GOODBYE FOREVER, WART!"

This SLY and Oh! So CLEVER Wart

That went EVERYWHERE with me!

It wasn't a WAIT AND GO AWAY WART

It wasn't a WASH AND WEAR AWAY WART

It wasn't a SCRUB AND DUB AWAY WART

15

This Mean and Green and Hateful wart

This Strange and Oh! So Spiteful Wart

This Seedy, Sickly, Sassy Wart

That went EVERYWHERE with me!

It stuck on tight with all its might

It got so that I couldn't write

It got so that I couldn't fight!

Now I don't think *that that* was right!

This Mean and Green and Hateful Wart

This Grimey, Slimey, Blimey Wart

This Throbbing, Bobbing, Brazen Wart

That went EVERYWHERE with me!

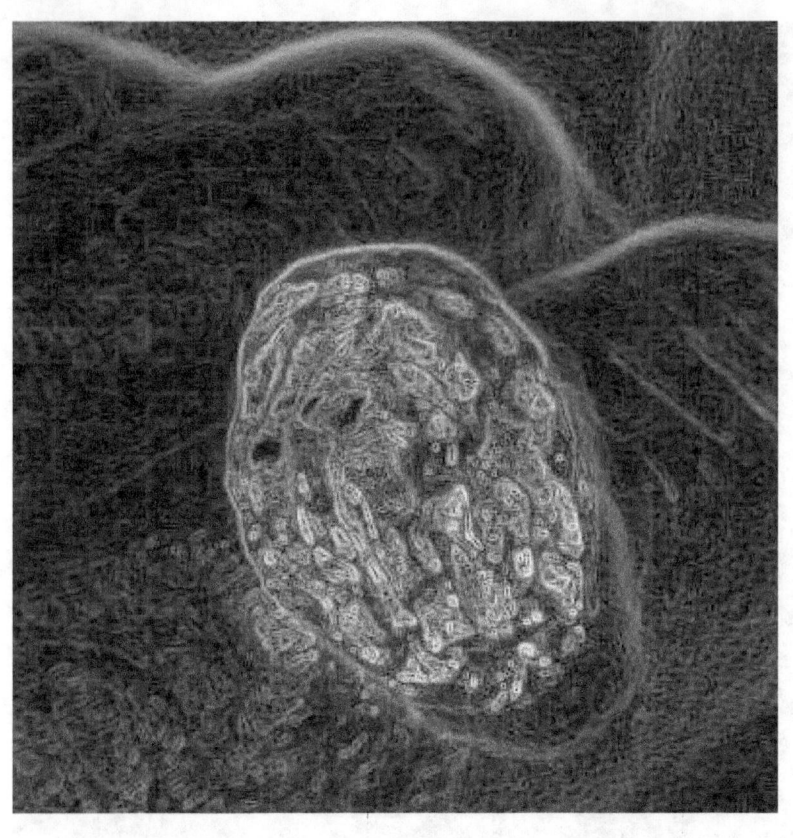

If it wasn't a WAIT AND GO AWAY WART

If it wasn't a WASH AND WEAR AWAY WART

If it wasn't a SCRUB AND DUB AWAY WART

THEN WHAT KIND OF WART WAS HE??!!!

For it stuck on tight with all its might

And looked real Scary in the night

Especially in the lantern light

As to Charmer's House I flee!

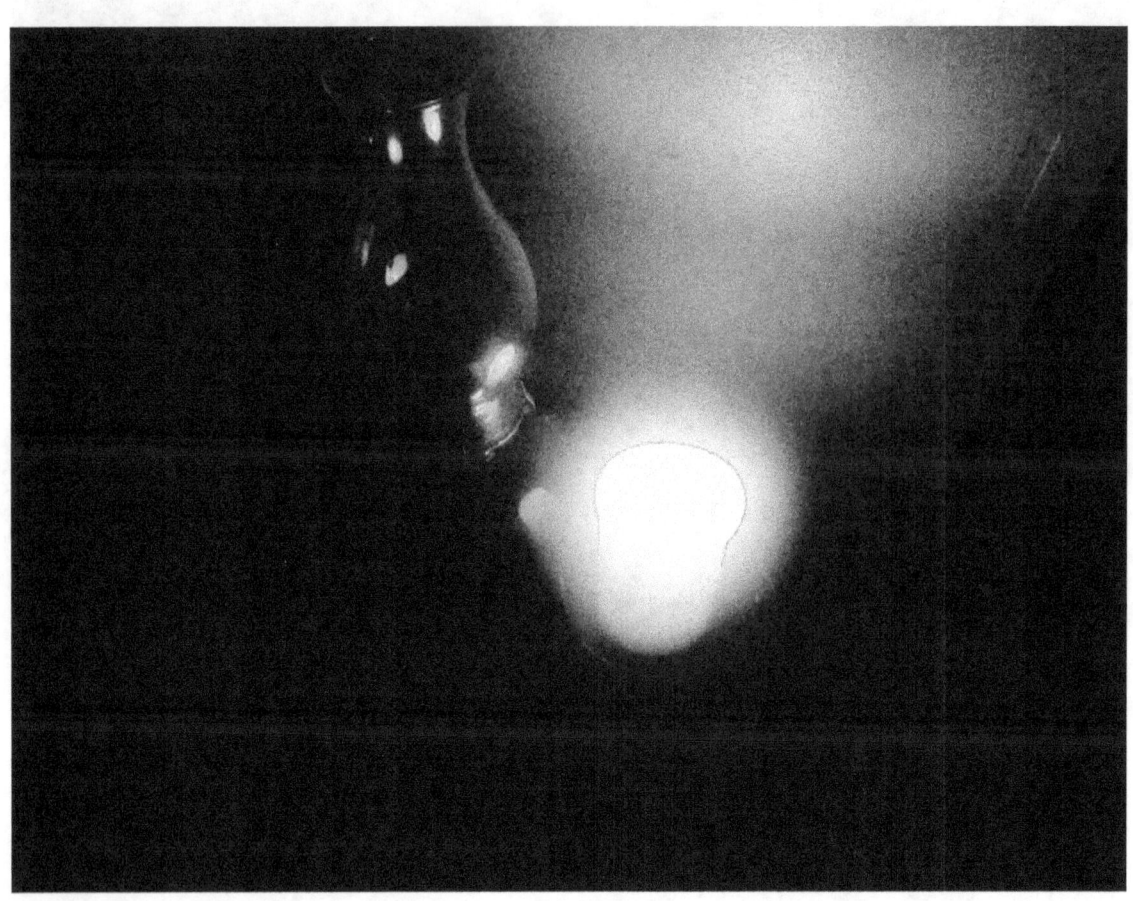

It was a House

A Homey House

A Musty, Misty, Gnomey House

This Charmer's House I see!

It was a House

A Charmer's House

An old and Wise old Farmer's House

A Musty, Misty, Magic House

This Eerie place I be!

With my Mean and Green and Hateful Wart

My Grimey, Slimey, Blimey Wart

My Throbbing, Bobbing, Knobbly, Wobbly,

Seedy, Sassy,

Sly and Bossy

Huge, Stuck-On-Forever Wart

That went EVERYWHERE with me!

It was a Charm

A curious Charm

That was wet and sticky on my arm

(But didn't do me any harm)

Just wrapped around my neck til dawn

And hid inside my sweating form

For three days secretly.

It was a Bog

A curious Bog

A Deep and Black and Sticky Bog

A Saggy, Scrunchy, Yicky Bog

Where I threw the Charm in glee!

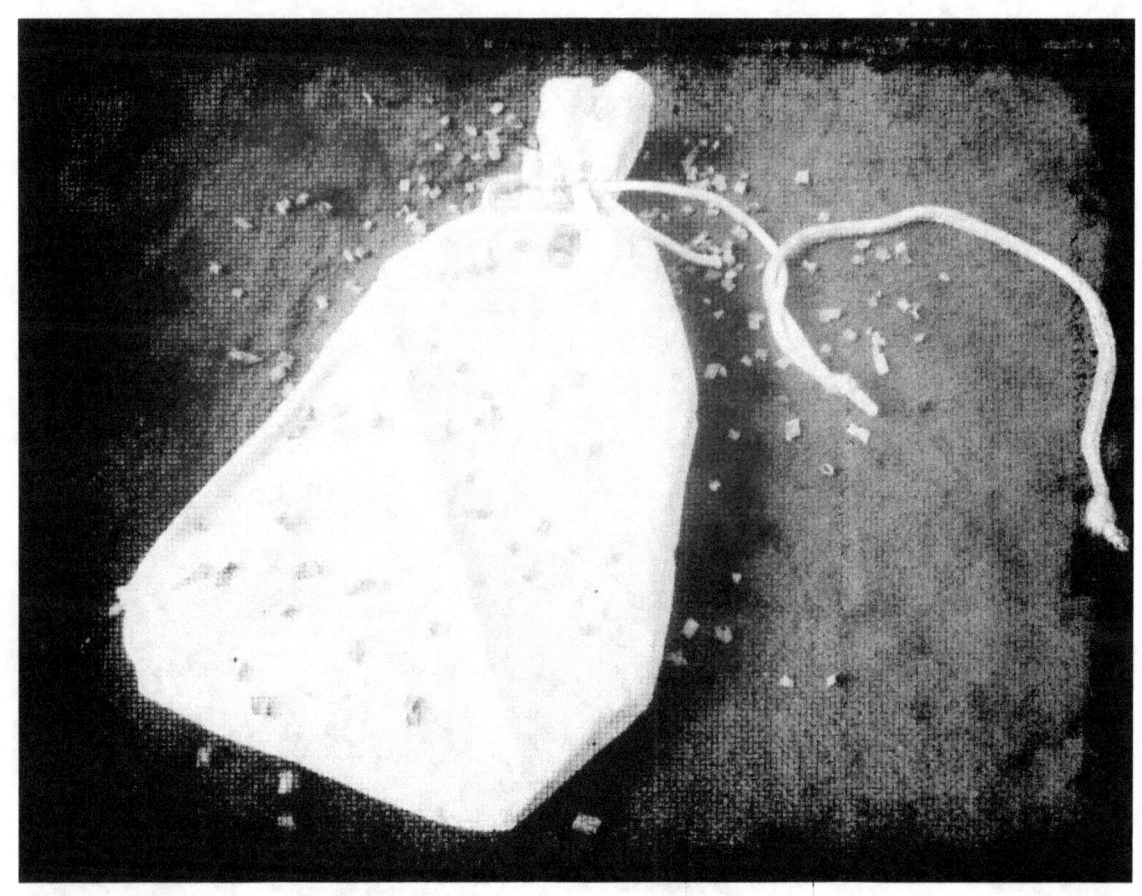

I had a Wart

An Ugly Wart

A Not So Very Funny Wart

THAT'S NEVER COMING BACK!!!

THE END.

About The Author

Geraldine Ryan Lush was born and raised in St. Joseph's, St. Mary's Bay,

NL. She received a B.A.(Ed.) from Memorial University, and taught school for a time. She is author of many books ranging from picture books to adult, including a collection of poetry. She has also published numerous scholarly articles on the children's literature field, in sources such as Books In Canada, The Newfoundland Quarterly and Canadian Children's Literature.   Her books have been widely reviewed in sources as School Library Journal, N.Y., Canadian Book Review Annual, Canadian Children's Literature, Quill & Quire, The Toronto Star, Winnipeg Free Press, Copley News Services, Washington, The Evening Telegram, many others. Her books, some in French translation, have been on the American Bookseller's Pick of the Lists, received the Merit Magazine Studio Award, Alcuin Society Design Award, Readers' Favourite 5-Star Award (honored by the American Library Association), and Atlantic Books Today Editors' Pick.   She lives in Mount Pearl.

Titles by Geraldine Ryan Lush:

-*The Gravel Pit Kids (Young Adult Novel)*

-*The Seashell's Lament (Adult Novel)*

-*Mrs. Clohiggledy's Clutter (All Ages)*

-*Hannigan's Hand (Paranormal Novel, YA-Adult)*

-*Hannigan's Hand: The Ghost Woman Talks (Paranormal Novel, YA-Adult)*

-*No Go Potty (Chapter Book, Malcolm K. Wall Series)*

-*Malcolm The Klutz (Chapter Books, Malcolm K. Wall Series)*

-*Malcolm And The Hamster Lady (Chapter Book (Malcolm*

K. Wall Series)

-Once When I Wasn't Looking (Poetry Collection, YA-Adult)

-Hairs On Bears (Picture Book)

-Jeremy Jeckles Hates Freckles (Picture/Storybook)

-Poils Poils Et Repoils (Picture Book)

-The Law-Breaking Adventures Of Teacher Tabitha (Middle Grade.) All Ages Appeal

-Haunted Towns: Ghost Stories From Newfoundland and Labrador. (Non-fiction collection of true ghost stories from across Newfoundland and Labrador).

Mqny other stories published in magazines and Newfoundland newspapers.

www.mulberrybooks.com   Facebook:
AuthorGeraldineRyanLush   @GRyanLush

Orders: www.amazon.com. www.amazon.ca. www.amazon.co.uk. www.amazon.id. www.chapters.indigo.ca. www.barnes&noble.com

To Order Directly And Save On Price And Shipping Contact: geraldine1942@live.com. Telephone: 709.368.5156. Facebook: AuthorGeraldineRyanLush

Twitter: @GRyanLush

Mulberry Books. 27-A Pasadena Cr. Suite 204. St. John's, NL . A1E4S4